TRAVELING THROUGH SPACE

John: It's up to us to save Western Civilization as we know it!

John

I am a fragment of rock thrown into space—Napoleon

TRAVELING THROUGH SPACE

John Lowry

iUniverse, Inc.
New York Lincoln Shanghai

TRAVELING THROUGH SPACE

Copyright © 2005 by John Lowry

All rights reserved. No part of this book may be used or reproduced by any means, graphic, electronic, or mechanical, including photocopying, recording, taping or by any information storage retrieval system without the written permission of the publisher except in the case of brief quotations embodied in critical articles and reviews.

iUniverse books may be ordered through booksellers or by contacting:

iUniverse
2021 Pine Lake Road, Suite 100
Lincoln, NE 68512
www.iuniverse.com
1-800-Authors (1-800-288-4677)

ISBN-13: 978-0-595-35806-9 (pbk)
ISBN-13: 978-0-595-80274-6 (ebk)
ISBN-10: 0-595-35806-3 (pbk)
ISBN-10: 0-595-80274-5 (ebk)

Printed in the United States of America

Thanks to the following publications in which the stories in this book have appeared, some in a slightly different form.

PRISM INTERNATIONAL: The Way It Always Is. Coney Island Shoot.

THE QUARTERLY: The Fifty and One Pleasures of Living. Falling. Out of the Blue. In Dorian's Office.

FICTION: The Temptation to Exist. Stout Robert. On Mars.

DESCANT: U-Turns. Life Stories.

CHICAGO REVIEW: Close. The Proposal.

HANGING LOOSE: Early Sunday Morning. Life is a Beach. The Easy Way.

CALIFORNIA QUARTERLY: Family. The Last Man.

ASPECT: Arlington.

NORTH AMERICAN REVIEW: Hawks. Little Darlings.

WRIT: Water Pump. Smiling Jack. Valued Customer. Traveling Through Space.

CITY COUNTRY MINERS: How to Play Hardball.

WORMWOOD REVIEW: Motion Picture.

CHIRON REVIEW: Here's Looking At You.

THE FIFTY AND ONE PLEASURES OF LIVING

When she comes
When she goes
You find ten dollars
It works
You didn't break it
Going away
Coming back
In bed with a cold
She gets on top
Wearing a bandage
The phone rings
The phone doesn't ring
The baby is sleeping
Rain on the window
It's not cancer
It's not you
Coming out of the water

New shoes
The cockatoo escapes
Watching a fight
Not getting into a fight
When the wheels touch the ground
You can hear everything
You get away with it
Finding your glasses
The door was locked
Before the movie starts
You don't need a haircut
It happens in another country
She follows you home
It didn't hurt
A train goes by
The fire is down the street
The old lady isn't your mother
You can stay another day
She stops crying
It isn't your fault
The suit fits
She takes the cat
You both have headaches
She takes off her earrings
A plane late at night
You were brave
They're not home
Watching her sleep
There's more
It goes away
It's early
It missed

Falling asleep
Waking up

THE WAY IT ALWAYS IS

I put the coffee on and looked out the window. The sky was clear with some puffy clouds. The cypress tree was in place on the corner, the apartment building across the street set for another day. Everything was just like yesterday.

Is this the way it always is? I said.

I took a shower. I shaved. First, the right side, then the left. Why didn't I ever start with the left side? I found shoes, shirts, a tie. Never found anything else, did I?

I went to the fruit store. I always went to the fruit store when the sky had puffy clouds. The fruit store had apples, oranges and bananas. I asked the lady for a Bodrick.

She smiled.

You know, fuzzy, like a peach but tasting more like an aardvark egg.

Her smile got broader.

Hell, they have them down the street.

She laughed.

I smiled, took my package and left. Why didn't I ever frown? When I got home, I thought, I'll look in the mirror, call myself an Elk turd and see if I frown.

I stopped. A man was looking at me. He wore a red jacket with gold braid around the buttons, blue pants and white shoes with bolts of lightning on them. He wore a rimless hat, like a fez, with a blue tassel. He pointed at me and laughed. I tapped my chest. Me? You're laughing at me? Yes, he was.

But I didn't keep his attention for long. Still laughing, he walked off, pointing to a tree, a car, a boy on a bicycle. Slowly, he raised his arms and looked towards the heavens.

LIFE STORIES

It was spring, the first warm day. We were waiting for the Whitney Museum to open. People were flying in every direction. Cabs played bumper car, bikers mowed down pedestrians, buses spread smoke like we were in a war zone. The semester was done, exams over.

We see a tall woman in a blue dress, short hair. She's carrying a Pekingese. We bow, smile. Madame, Burt says, am I correct in saying your husband imports antiques from main land China? And that the townhouse you own in the East sixties used to belong to Montgomery Clift? The woman smiles, shakes her head. We fall in beside her. Ah, come on, we say. We're young, intoxicated by life. We'll never be this happy again. It's so obvious, she says. I'm a veterinarian. Pooky is dying of leukemia. I'm taking her for a walk. She loves Madison Avenue. We consider Pooky. My turtles always died, Burt says. We stop at the corner. The woman waves. My husband was in the import business. Cars

We go back to the Museum. A plump woman is standing in our spot. Thick glasses, a shopping bag, a book with a comb as a place mark. Hi, Burt says, you're a retired secretary. You're visiting the Museum to keep sharp and current. Wrong, I say. I'm perceptive enough to see you're reading a book about Pablo Picasso's sex life. You're a scholar, probably teach at NYU. You're writing a book so you can get tenure and never have to work again. You remind me of my patients, the woman says. I'm a psychiatrist, Director of Healing-In-Arts. We teach poetry and music to drug addicts to reawaken their oneness with the world. I'm waiting for my friend. She was a brilliant dancer, a brilliant stage manager.

She's had a series of psychotic episodes. On a day like this, I say? How about the book? Oh, my secretary gave it to me.

The woman opens her book, holds the comb in her mouth. We spot a tall guy in a thousand dollar suit. He's big shouldered, his wavy hair streaked with gray. Retired general, I say. Got his knee shot off in Nam, got a great pension. Actor, Burt says. Those teeth are so bonded he looks like a racehorse. I run after him. Excuse me sir, I say. My friend and I are interviewing passersby to see why they are passersby. You are a retired Colonel. You do consulting work for companies that make explosives. The guy stares straight ahead. My therapist says I'm too young for life, if that's any help. We were close to the corner, the line of demarcation. The guy stops, looks down at his shoes. I was a downhill skier, he says. Won the bronze in the 1976 Olympics. I had money, cars, women. I drank, did coke. I married a rich woman. It's all gone now. She threw me out. I have arthritis, constant pain from the pins and bolts in my legs. I'm walking, he shrugged, just to be walking. Gee, I said, if there's anything I can do. The guy shakes his head. I own two condominiums; I have thousands in a Swiss bank account. I've always been a complaining, self-pitying bastard. Talking to you has been a pleasure.

I get back to the Museum. Burt is talking to a girl. She's pretty, dark hair, cat eyes. She walks off laughing. Isn't she beautiful, Burt says? She could be a model but she's a writer. She's getting a book published. His eyes are glazed. What happened to the lady? I say. Burt came into focus. Yeah, her friend, the crazy dancer? It's a he. He's half her age, looks like something out of GQ. She lied? I say. Burt nodded. It's getting harder and harder to have faith in people.

People were streaming into the Museum. Want to see the show? I say. Burt nodded. The dreamy look had come back. A pizza truck pulled up in a No Standing Under Penalty of Death zone. A guy gets out wearing a white jump suit. He's balding, goateed. You look like good guys, he says, you watch my truck? Drive it around the block if the cops come? Sure, I say, we're dumb enough to do that. He tosses me the keys. You're delivering lunch, I say. It's Friday, people think, what the hell, I'll eat pizza, take the risk of going into a cholesterol coma. And you're illegal, Burt says. Mexican, right? Hey, you got my respect. You work hard. You send money to your family. The guy glares, wants his keys. I'm a painter, he says. I deliver pizza, I drive a cab, I work in a health club. Whatever it takes. My girlfriend does word processing all night for an insurance company. She hates it, but she does it for me. For us. I paint all day, all night. I never sleep. I'm good, he says, pointing to the Museum. I'll be in here some day and guys like you will go around with earphones stuck in your head trying to understand it. I shake my head. I'm simple, I say, but this is the worst yet. Yeah, Burt said, he's going to be a doctor and he's totally insensitive. Me, I'm into microeconomics. I think art is something that goes on a calendar. The guy smiles, tosses back the keys. No sweat. I'll be right out. I just want a minute of greatness.

The pretty girl makes another go-round. Wow, Burt says, this is it! He falls in beside her. I'm dull but a plodder, he says, I want kids, a home, a completely uneventful life. She sticks her cute chin in the air. They walk to the corner. Burt stops a cab. He waves, signals to me. Burt, I yell, see if she's got a sister!

I'm mad. I should have told her I was going to be a doctor. A guy stops, looks at me. He's short, wispy gray hair. Hey, he says, what a great face, full of sadness and angst. Let me guess. You're best buddy just stole your girl. You're thinking of walking to the river, staring down at the water, getting wrecked in some cheap bar. Right? Don't weird-off with me, I say.

The pizza guy comes out, I toss him the keys. Great, he says. I can do that. Man, I'm going to be rich, I'm going to be famous. He jumps into his truck, toots his horn. I look at the Museum. There's a beautiful artist, sensitive, lonely. Rich. I'll walk up, full of sadness and angst. What the hell.

FALLING

I was sick of it. It was all boring. I opened a window, looked at my dog and jumped. Falling was cool, refreshing. My arms and legs opened. I overtook a woman. She was falling like a pole, her arms pinned to her sides, hair flying. She was pretty. Our eyes met. We smiled. Our lips moved, but we could hear nothing. We caught up to a falling house. It was pretty. It had a green roof, red shutters, a lawn. We landed on the lawn. There was a wind like a hurricane. We fought our way into the house and slammed the door. We started to speak. We were shouting. I love you, I said. I'm Katherine, she said. I love you too. We kissed. We made love in front of the hearth. After, we explored our house. It was comfortable and had spare bedrooms. We were still falling. We could see clouds rushing past, hear the wind. Katherine made dinner. The wind calmed. We went outside. There were stars. We smelled flowers, heard crickets. A gentle breeze stirred the trees. We've stopped falling, I said. Life is normal again, Katherine said. We slept well. The morning was sunny. Birds sang near the window. After breakfast, I went out to the garage. There was a car. I got in, waved to Katherine, drove to work. I whistled as I drove. I felt happy. I got to the office and waited for the elevator. When the door opened, I got on. But there was no car. I was falling. It was black and damp smelling. My arms and legs flew open. I thought of my dog.

OUT OF THE BLUE

We had just finished dinner when we heard a small sound in our garden. Something had fallen. I went to the window. My God, I cried, there's someone there!

We ran outside. A young man lay on the grass, his limbs every which way. He had thick hair. A piece of bone stuck up through the knee of his jeans. Mary knelt down. Poor boy, she said, touching his hair. He was dead.

I helped Mary up.

What can we do, I said?

We stood a moment.

So terrible, Mary said.

We waited for the authorities. When they did not come, we turned on the television. There was no news. Nothing had crashed. There had been no explosions. In the morning, I said. But our doorbell did not ring. We went outside.

Mary sobbed, wrung her hands.

Time went by. Our daughter had a baby. I took a leave from work. A violent storm left us without lights for ten days. Each morning we went to the window. The boy had sunk into the earth. Some leaves covered the spot. The piece of bone stuck up like a marker. After a while, it disappeared. There was nothing to be seen. We stopped going to the window.

One night, when the first snowstorm blew against the house, we sat reading. Mary put down her book. She pressed her hands to her temples.

What is it? I said.

This sadness, she said. My heart just sinks. Out of the blue.

Yes, I said. Yes.

THE TEMPTATION TO EXIST

Charles exercised every morning. He had green eyes, a long nose. He was tall and strong, a man with reserves, a member of a small, profitable law firm. He was twenty-eight years old.

He shared an office with Nancy Rowe and Dennis Hartley. Nancy had prominent cheek bones. She wore dark suits and simple blouses, double rows of pearls, a single gold chain. Her husband was a psychologist. Charles overheard their low, whispered quarrels on the phone.

Dennis rode a motorcycle. He lived with an actress who had been in two movies. He was pale, his face round, his lank hair almost colorless. When I make mine, he said, I'm opening a brewery. And I'm going to be a dancer, Nancy said, spinning in her chair. And you, Charles dear? What do you want out of life? He pretended to consider. Whatever is there?

Not for me, Charles thought on the train. Screaming babies. Petty arguments at breakfast. The same face, day after day, more wrinkled, more disappointed. No, not for me, he thought, smiling.

Just before nine each evening, he sat with a Scotch and called his mother. She lived in Maine with three dogs and a shotgun. She passed her days painting, her evenings with bourbon and television. I wish I had more money, Charles. Why mother? Why? To be better than everyone else, of course. That poor man never enjoyed his money. He was so afraid of what people thought. That poor man, his father, who walked into the woods and shot himself on Christmas morning. Will

I see you while I'm still lucid, Charles? As soon as I clear my calendar, mother. Well, bring a cannon or something. There are too many trees. He was in bed by eleven, falling asleep immediately. He never remembered dreaming.

His phone rang when he was rowing. It was Rip, the office manager. How's about tooling up to Rochester, Charles? When? How's about today? He hated travel. The crowded planes, hotel rooms with their canned air, paintings of ducks and rowboats. He sat by a window, his arms folded, eyes closed, waiting for take-off. A fat man collapsed into his seat, startling him. Charles opened his eyes. A woman stood by the emergency door. She had black hair, a fine jaw, dark blue eyes. She was beautiful. His heart seemed to swing loose in his chest. The woman returned his gaze, smiling slightly before sealing the door and walking off.

When the plane reached altitude, Charles opened his laptop and began studying the case of Jackson Molloy vs. Jenny Molloy, oddly distracted by the sound of every woman's voice.

He caught a glimpse of her as they filed off the plane. She was in the cockpit, laughing, trying on a pilot's sunglasses. Well, so much for that, Charles thought, walking briskly to the taxi station, passing two red caps who were joking about a dead man who had arrived at the airport in a taxi.

He checked into his room, sitting down at the desk with his laptop, his depositions. From time to time, he stretched, walking to the window. The street was dark. A red light flashed in what looked like a park. When he finished, he put on his jacket and took the elevator to the lobby.

The Metro bar was dark, cool. Couples sat at candle lit tables. A man in a white jacket pressed soft chords on a piano. Rows of glasses reflected brilliantly in the bar mirror. A football in a plastic case stood behind the cash register. A Scotch, neat, Charles said, sitting down. A deeply tanned man sat in a corner, snapping his fingers softly to the music. Three people came in, laughing and shoving one another. They wore uniforms and carried shoulder bags. Charles watched in the mirror as one of the women took off her cap, shaking out her dark hair. It was the woman from the plane. She was talking rapidly, gesturing, making her friends laugh. Charles took a sip of his drink. He felt excited, on the verge of taking some action, when the woman got up and walked to the bar. She was unsteady in her high heels, the corners of her mouth working. Cap, she said to the bartender, we going to get service or we call out the militia? She noticed Charles. Hi there, you look familiar. You work for John Deere? Cute lady, the man said, watching her walk away. But oh, can she drink.

That night Charles sat up in bed. Someone tumbled against his door, laughing and shaking the knob. He sat listening as the person shuffled down the hall, singing *Julie Blue Eyes* in a croaking voice. He lay awake, thinking of high school, a short assertive girl from the tennis team. He had pulled his car onto a dirt road and they had made love, a dog barking in a darkened house.

He had breakfast in the SunRise Nook. Couples sat staring into space, reading newspapers. A man in a jogging suit cut a doughnut into six pieces, eating them with a pensive expression.

Jackson Molloy sat behind his desk. Cans of paint on a side table were stacked into a pyramid. His humped back and hooded eyes put Charles in mind of a captive bird. His daughter Jenny had fled to Mexico with her personal trainer and two hundred thousand dollars. Why? Molloy asked, turning out his hands. Is it something she didn't have? Is it something I didn't do?

Charles made an early flight to New York. A two engine-plane sat on the tarmac, a stripe on its side ending in a lightning bolt. He remembered flying his model planes over the football field, his father watching their low, uneven loops, explaining what it was like to be shot down over Vietnam. He could resist no longer and turned towards the emergency door. A red faced man, his cap at a jaunty angle, stood greeting passengers.

Rip sat scowling at the front desk when Charles came in. Call me when Sidney is free, he said, flipping through his messages. Nancy saw him coming. I have to go, she said, banging down the phone. She sat a moment with her eyes closed, her hands squeezing her cheeks. Charles, she said, Dennis has been in an accident. Did anyone say anything? Charles shook his head. He ran his bike under a truck. He's paralyzed. She flushed, seized her purse and ran down the corridor. Charles sat staring at a picture taken at Fire Island. Dennis was laughing, holding his girl friend on his shoulders, her hands over his eyes. His phone rang. He's all yours, bub, Rip said.

Sidney waved him to a chair. He was signing papers, tossing them one by one into his out basket. A small television on a corner of his desk flashed stock quotations. His face, long, hard as a biscuit, was sunburned from days spent steering a ninety foot sloop through the waters of Long Island. He sighed, tossing his pen aside. You heard about Dennis? Yes. But paralyzed? Charles said. Charlie, Sidney said, guys who ride motorcycles want to raise hell. They might even be lawyers but they want to raise hell. These doctors, he went on, waving dismissively, they watch too much television. Hell, he'll walk. He'll be OK. Maybe he'll limp. What's a limp? He leaned forward, narrowing his pale eyes. It scares you. Right? But Charlie, it's good. It's drama. It's life. Sure, sure it is. The television caught his attention and he frowned. Now look at that crap for God's sake. He shrugged. OK, let's talk Jackson Molloy.

Nancy was standing by the elevator when Charles walked up. Where is this friggin' thing, she said, slapping the button. They got on and Nancy leaned against the wall, one leg thrust out. Maybe it's not so bad, Charles said. She nodded and began to cry. Oh Charlie, I'm so scared! He took a step towards her and she threw out her arms. They embraced, briefcases swinging, pressing to one another until the car reached the lobby. Rip stood waiting, holding a bag of doughnuts. Enjoy the trip, guys? Oh boy, Nancy said, hurrying off.

Charles poured a Scotch and called his mother. Charles, you're early, she said. Is anything wrong? Are you with a woman? I just have this sense when a woman is involved. Mother, he said, I'm thinking of existing. There was a pause. Of course you exist, Charles. What are you talking about? I mean existing the way other people exist. But I'm afraid it's terrible. Is it terrible, mother? She laughed, that stranger's laugh that frightened him when he was a boy. Why Charles, no. You just pretend. That's all. If you can't, you make a lot of money.

THE PROPOSAL

One afternoon, she came to his door.
    I admire you, she said. I like your driving, your shoulders. You smile sparingly and only work for money. You cut wood and like animals.
    Listen, she said, marry me this afternoon. We'll have lunch in the best restaurant and honeymoon in an apartment with a garden. We'll have sex then and only then. You'll have all the money you want. Do what you please but when I call you must come. Take three minutes to decide.
    He said yes and they were happy for many years

U-TURNS

The Post Office was crowded. They put out metal posts with soft ropes. The line snaked around them, making u-turns.

I walked around the first post and faced the line coming up. There was this cute girl. She wore thin glasses, had a sweet face, soft skin. It moves fast, I said. There's no one here after three o'clock, she said. I smiled. She smiled.

I made my first u-turn. This tall girl, long hair, green eyes, was passing on my left. I smiled. She gave me her North Atlantic salmon look. Beats working, I said, shrugging. A guy was yelling behind me. I turned. We here for stamps or sexual encounters of the worst kind? he said. He wore a hat pushed back on his head, his eyes bugging out. Who are you, the Postmaster General? I shot back. He was standing next to a woman with squinty eyes and blond hair that looked like it had been borrowed from a broom. She gave me a sour look.

The cute girl and I met again. A girl like you must have hundreds of boy-friends, right? Her cheeks colored. And you're married, right, live in Scarsdale? I shook my head. Columbus Avenue, I said. Five floor walk-up. Her eyes opened. Where? I told her. She lived four blocks away. We went to the same movie, the same coffee bar.

Another U. The tall girl was three people from the flashing green arrow. Excuse me, I said to the woman in front of me. She had a shopping bag full of papers in her arms, wore a hat that looked like a flowerpot turned upside down. Men are such bastards, she said, but since this was a public space she had no grounds for legal action at the present time. Thank you, I said. I'm in love with you, I said to the tall girl, I'm going to marry you. She said something. Sorry, I said? She said it again. It sounded like Czech or German. The green arrow came on and she walked to a window. There's a Berlitz school right around the corner, flowerpot said.

The guy was yelling again, tapping his watch. What are you, a sexual predator? Who the hell are you, I said, my father? If I were your father, you wouldn't be here, he said. People laughed. Damn.

I was first in line. What was I here for anyway? The cute girl came up. We're in love, I said, you don't know it yet, but we are. Please don't patronize me, she said. I'm just as capable of recognizing love as you are. Good, I said, good for you. The guy was screaming again, waving his arms. You must live alone with a cat and a can of tuna fish, I said. People laughed. All right.

I got the green arrow. I passed the tall woman as she turned away from the window. *Quel belle mademoiselle*, I said. She was fooling with her stamps and ignored me. I asked the clerk for today's special. Some matinee idol with curly hair called out, opened his arms. The cute girl ran off the line, kissed his cheeks. Probably her brother.

I headed for the door. The squinty-eyed woman grabbed my arm, handed me a card. Lisa Montel, it said, Exotic Body Massage.

CLOSE

I was glad to be home. It had been close.
Were you scared? she asked.
No.
Did anyone scream?
I don't think so.
What did you think about?
I tried to remember.
Nothing, really.
She smiled, fooling with a spoon.
How's Tommy? I asked.
Fine.
And Debbie?
The same as always.
Any rain?
Not a drop.
I smiled and reached for my coffee.
Was it horrible? she asked.
Not really.

EARLY SUNDAY MORNING

It was early, a June morning and I took a stroll for the paper. Hardly anyone was around.

After a few blocks, I saw a guy cross the street reading a newspaper. A car turned the corner and hit him. He rolled up the hood, bounced off the windshield and fell off, still holding the paper. The driver opened the door.

You OK?

The guy was kneeling in the street. He nodded, got up and walked away. He started reading the paper again.

Down the street, in the window of a brownstone, I saw two guys dancing, holding each other at arm's length. The piano was loud, like a ballet class. A little kid and a big dog were standing in front of the next house. The dog had blue eyes, the kid had blue eyes. The kid growled at me.

I got the paper, some milk and came home a different route. Big clouds came over rooftops. Birds darted around.

A woman opened the door of a house. She was naked. She had a big belly and large breasts. Her hair was pulled off her neck and she had a plate in her hand covered with plastic.

Pauli, she called, looking at me without interest. Pauli, it's time for your tuna fish.

I walked on.

FAMILY

When I came home, Caesar, our Labrador, came running to the door. He barked twice. He wagged his tail twice. I patted him on the head. He barked again and sat down, looking at the door. My son came toddling up. Scott, I said, Scotty. Scotty grabbed my pants and looked up at me. His eyes were shining.

Daddy, I love you, he said. Daddy, will you play with me?

I patted him on the head.

Daddy, he said, will you read to me?

My wife came out of the kitchen. She smiled. She kissed me. She opened her blouse and showed me her breasts.

You want sex, dear?

Yes, later, I said. You want a drink? she said. You want dinner, dear?

Yes, I would like a drink, I said. But I would like a bath. Would you draw it for me?

Of course, dear.

She went upstairs. Scotty was sitting on the couch watching television. I turned it on for him. I called Caesar from the door. Caesar, play with Scotty, I said. The dog jumped up on the couch and licked Scotty's cheek.

I went upstairs and undressed in the bedroom. I put on a bathrobe and went to the bathroom. My bath was ready. Martha had my martini. She was smiling. She opened her blouse and showed me her breasts.

You want sex dear?

Yes, later, I said.

She smiled. She said she would make dinner. She went downstairs.

I got into the tub. The water was perfect. I sipped my martini. It was perfect. I closed my eyes. Jim loves Martha, I said. Jim loves Scotty and Caesar.

ARLINGTON

Years ago, I lived in Arlington, Virginia. A nice place. I had a house, a job, a new car. I was happy. Tree shaded streets, kids on bikes delivering the Sunday paper. And it was clean.

One morning, the guy across the street, a doctor, got a new television. I saw it sitting in his driveway. It was peculiar because there was no crate; it just sat outside, the way it would in your living room. It rained that afternoon. No one came out for the TV. It just got rained on.

It was still there the next morning. People noticed it. I got calls, the doctor got calls. Yes, he said, he knew the TV was there; no, he wasn't concerned. Actually, it was no one's business. I could see him from my kitchen, goateed and stooped, puttering around in his examining room.

The TV stayed put. Day after day, rain, wind, snow. Every morning, over coffee I had the same thought: look at that expensive television, rotting. Sometimes I took out my binoculars. For a long while, it looked as good as new, except for some bird droppings on the cabinet but, gradually, it aged. The cabinet turned a dull white. Something peeled off the metal binding around the tube. It was fascinating, watching it die. Summer and it hung on. People got mad at the doctor. There was talk about eyesores and legal redress but nothing came of it.

One evening, feeling gloomy over the extraction of two molars, I went to my window with a drink. Son of a gun, the tube had sunk in the cabinet, like a cock-eyed sunset. Total collapse was imminent, by morning perhaps. But it didn't happen for three months. Altogether, a year had gone by. I had gotten married.

The tube was taken for granted and for a long while it remained unchanged. One morning, my wife ran into our bedroom.

It's gone! she cried. It's fallen apart!

She was right. Tubes, colored wires were all over the driveway. The same day, two guys came in a truck, picked up the pieces, swept the driveway and drove off. The only thing left was some kind of stain, as though it had bled.

A month or so later, my wife was talking to me on the phone when she paused. Her voice grew tense. What? What was it? A huge, beautiful grandfather clock was being delivered to the doctor. There was no packing case.

I left the office. At home, my wife was crying. I ran to the window. Jesus Christ! It was in the driveway. I slammed the window shut.

Oh God, no!

He can't, my wife said.

The clock is still there. It's in great shape. It will last a long time.

HAWKS

The car shook on the dirt road. I hope they don't come, Jill said. I want to be alone. It's either them or no house, Tal said. The house appeared, a pine tree in front, green shingled, robed in a white balcony. There was no car.

A damp, musty smell swept past when they opened the door. Sunlight lit the living room, showing orange cracks in the leather couch, bald patches on the rug. A child's wooden train was drawn up in a circle.

They walked onto the deck. Vin's a hunter, Jill said. He kills innocent animals. Puffy clouds, dark bellied, floated on the horizon. There were soft crickets, the flapping of wings. Look! Jill said. Two birds, their wings motionless, circled over the house. Hawks, she said, smiling. Great, Tal said. Want to play tennis?

The Murphy's car pulled up to the tennis court as they began to play. Tal and Jill waved as they walked towards them. It's so hot in the city, they're frying eggs on car hoods again, Isabel said. She had been an actress. She was blond, small featured, like a child. We're staying forever, Jill said. Vincent was thin, dark, his eyes gleaming and nervous. He was an assistant district attorney. I brought work, he said. My pleasure will be in not doing it. They turned back to their car. Catch you at the house.

Disappointed? Tal said. We expected them didn't we? Jill said. Exactly. Isabel is pretty though, isn't she? she said. She's really all right, Tal said. Oh is she? Jill said. And how all right is that?

Isabel was watching television when they walked in, her legs crossed, her hair pulled off her neck. A rifle sheathed in a leather case stood in the foyer. Did I tell

- 24 -

you I might resume my career? she said, waving dramatically. Really? Tal said. Yes. Last week I read for Robert Redford's agent. And he liked me. I told him, I'll do anything but just because God made me a blond doesn't mean he made me dumb. Look at that, Jill said. The television showed bodies floating down a river, a crowd watching from the shore. What is that? Isabel said. Mozambique, Jill said. There's a civil war. Vin came down the stairs and froze when he saw the television. Blow the place up, he said. I hate this, Tal said, I'm going to wash up. Isabel snapped off the television and walked to the kitchen. Jill, you and Tal want to join us for lunch? That would be nice, let me help, Jill said, pinning back her dark hair. Vin made a gesture. And me? You, Isabel said, you light the barbecue and don't burn down the house.

I'd love to teach, have the summers off, Isabel said, opening the refrigerator. What do you do? I read, I write, Jill said, taking plates from the cupboard. You writing a best seller? I write poetry, Jill said, blushing. I used to love to read, Isabel said. And now? I live the stupid life. The stupid television, the stupid VCR. She peeled open a package of frankfurters. Tal came into the kitchen, his hair damp, his sallow skin glowing. Tal, Isabel said, Vin's a pyromaniac. Would you see what's he's doing?

The barbecue was set on the end of the deck. Vin stood waving a piece of tinfoil over the coals. Fanning the flames, hey Mr. District Attorney? Tal said. Heat is what I do best, Vin said, reaching for the charcoal lighter. Tal blocked his hand. Hey, let it alone! You got it going. Vin smiled. Corporate lawyers, you guys oil your shoes.

Jill here has the whole summer off, Isabel said at the table. Hey, Vin said, go for it. Of course, I got secretaries who can't spell. I had one who never heard of Michigan. Jill peered at him over her glasses. Maybe. But did you ever notice how many Wall Street crooks have degrees from Ivy League schools? Vin shrugged. Just telling you the facts of life. It all comes down to morality, Tal said. Values and decency.

Isabel patted her napkin to her mouth. When I started driving up here, she said. People were waving. Honking. I'm like, is my car on fire? Did I forget my clothes? Then I think, my God, they're just being friendly. Isabel, Tal said, you'll wake up tonight. I guarantee it. You'll say, what's wrong? There's not a ghost? Isabel said. I'm terrified of ghosts. Tal shook his head. No, Isabel, the silence. The first night we stayed up here, I heard something. What's that? I thought. You know what it was, Isabel? A frog, way over on the lake, just showing off. Now that's silence, Tal concluded, leaning back into his chair. And today, we saw hawks, Jill said, making wings of her arms. Just wheeling through the sky, princes of the sun. You guys ski? Vin said, forking another frankfurter. You hunt? Absolutely not, Jill said. Hunting is immoral. Vin cringed in mock fear. I think it's OK if the herds get too big, Isabel said. Vin looked up at the sky. Want to hit a few tennis balls, Tal? You bet, Tal said. If you like, Isabel, we can take a walk, Jill said. Isabel hesitated. There aren't any snakes? No snakes, Tal promised but wear your jeans and boots. There are ticks.

Two women wearing dresses and baseball caps were on the court, laughing and swinging their rackets like baseball players. Must be nuns, Tal said, leaning against the fence. We talking softball? Vin said. God, they're old. So what? Tal said. So what, Vin said, I'm making peanuts, that's what. I should get old? I should retire? Where? Sheepshead Bay? Greater Flushing? So quit, Tal said. Come over to my place. Yeah? Vin said. How about Jill? Your kids? Who's going to protect them from the predators? The women waved them onto the court. Have it your way, Tal said. Let's play tennis.

Vin floated the ball over the baseline, made short returns that Tal smashed for winners. Tal served rows of aces and spun a second serve that rode in on Vin's racket. Vin's serve fell long. When he double faulted, he shouted, banging his racket down on the court. After he won the set, Tal walked to the net. I've been playing a lot, Vin. Don't give me that boy scout crap, Vin said, his face flushed. Just play.

Vin's serve began to catch the corners. He rushed the net, putting away Tal's weak returns. Tal waved his racket. You're foot-faulting, he said. Vin cupped his hand to his ear. What? They walked towards one another. You're on the court before you hit the ball. A foot fault, Tal explained. What the hell you saying? Vin said. I'm just playing better. You got a problem with that? If I lose, Tal said, pointing his finger, I lose by the rules. No other way. Vin walked away, then whirled around. You want to play? Play it is, Tal said. Vin won the set, raising his arms in the air. Nice going, Tal said.

Tal drove slowly, humming to a cassette of the New World Symphony. Vin sat with his eyes closed, his arms folded. You guys want to see a movie tonight? he said. Tal slammed on the brakes. Look at that! A faun stood by the road, moving his head from side to side before catching their scent and bounding off. Oh man! Tal said, I wish Jill was here. He started the car. How can people shoot them? How can they do it? I'm a hunter, Vin said, I don't shoot fauns. Small favors, Tal replied. They pulled up to the house. Vin clapped him on the back. No hard feelings, bud? Tal stared at him. Sure, I was foot-faulting. But I was losing man. It's just a game.

Jill sat reading on the deck. So, how was tennis? she said. Tal sat down. The guy cheats, he said in a low voice. Mr. District Attorney cheats at tennis. Jill lowered her book. He told her what had happened. And wait, there's more. In the car, he tells me, sure I was foot-faulting. But it's just a game. He plucked at the strings of his racket. Hope your walk was better. Jill rolled her eyes. You told Isabel to wear jeans and boots? How about shorts and sandals? All she did was complain. Something is biting me, something is on me. Tal told her about the faun. Oh Tal, can we go back? Maybe he'll come again. Sure we can, Tal said. A full moon, the color of a plum, rose over the hills. They watched it climb past pickerel clouds, warming to the incandescence of candlelight. Tal, I'm so happy, Jill said. Are you? Very, he said, taking her hand and kissing it.

She lay in his arms, stroking his cheek. Let's not tell them our plans, she said. Suppose they build next to us? No way, Tal said, kissing her shoulder, dropping the strap of her nightgown. She turned, kissing him passionately. A car pulled up and they made furtive love, listening to the Murphys tramp up the stairs, arguing in animated whispers. Jill closed her eyes. A white hawk dropped towards her, his eyes the color of fall.

There were steps in the hall, a sharp rap on the door. Tal, wake up! Vin called. We got a prowler. They put on their robes and Tal opened the door. Vin stood in camouflage pants and t-shirt, holding his rifle, Isabel behind him in a football jersey. Someone's on the deck, he said. You hear it? A raccoon, I bet, Tal said, pushing the rifle aside. Yeah, but I'm not a betting man, Vin said. They went downstairs. No lights, Vin ordered.

They stood by the kitchen window. Tables and chairs levitated in the moon light, falling into place when they glanced away. There, Tal said, pointing. A dark form held something that flashed like a signal lamp. Some bum? Vin said. A bear, Tal said, chuckling. Isabel suppressed a cry. He likes our tinfoil. He opened the door. Hah! he shouted, waving his arms. Hah! The bear ran into the shadows. Vin slammed the door. You nuts? We don't want him in here! He'll go away, Jill said, he's just hungry. And suppose he doesn't? Vin said, wheeling. Suppose he gets in here in the middle of the night? They don't do that, Jill said. They're shy. Should we fire a warning shot? Isabel said. Vin hesitated, his eyes darting around.

Oh, for God's sake! Tal said, opening the door and stepping onto the deck. Jill called after him sharply. He walked rapidly, throwing back his shoulders, stopping when he heard a growl. The bear was curled against a corner of the deck. Tal raised his arms. Git! Git! The bear dropped his head to one side, baring his teeth and coming towards him. Tal felt a flush of heat. He turned and ran. He saw a flash, heard the side of the house explode. He looked back and saw the bear somersault through the air.

Vin walked towards him, lowering his rifle. That sucker was going to kill you. Tal tried to catch his breath. They walked to the bear, Vin pointing his rifle. He lay on his back, small moons swimming in his eyes.

Isabel threw herself at Vin when they came into the kitchen. Where's Jill? Tal said. She shook her head. He bounded up the stairs. We gotta talk, Vin called. This is going to be trouble.

She was lying on the bed. Tal stood a moment, wiping the sweat from his face. Jill, he said, sitting down. She averted her face. It was an old bear. He was sick. That's why he came around. He touched her shoulder. Jill, please! She sprang from the bed and stood trembling. I don't know you! she cried. I don't know you!

LIFE IS A BEACH

As usual, I left for work in the middle of something important. Claire was talking about taxes. I came back and tapped on the kitchen window. She looked startled.

I'm sorry, I said when she opened it. I always leave when you want to talk.

Is something wrong? she said. Are you seeing someone?

I drove to the Expressway, stopping near the token booth. The sky was hazy. There was an ozone alert. Air quality was unhealthy. I got out and lit a cigarette. Sorry, I said, but I'm tapering off.

The red BMW came along. I waved him down. The driver was a shadow behind the darkened glass. He cracked the window and kept the motor running.

It's me, I said, pointing to my car. Silver Mustang. Every morning, I cut you off here. Every morning we race to the bridge. I always win, always give you the finger. I'm sorry. It's all so stupid.

The window snapped shut. BMW blasted off, cutting in front of a woman in a Saab.

I pulled into my office garage. The guy came out of his glass house, followed by his big dog.

Morning, I said.

I never said good morning.

The guy stopped. The dog growled.

I extended my hand.

Five years and I still don't know your name.

Charlie, he said.

Nice dog you got there, Charlie.

I handed him ten dollars. He stood looking at the money.

All these years, I said. I never gave you a tip.

Charlie nodded.

All these years, he said, I've been siphoning gas from your tank.

In the office, I told the Spanish receptionist that I was sorry I had made fun of her mustache. She said something real fast in Spanish. A typist translated. She said she is sorry too that she made fun of your big butt.

My partner Marty was on the phone to L.A. He winked when I came into his office. I took out the check and placed it on his desk. He raised his eyebrows when he saw the amount. He put his hand over the phone.

For what?

You don't want to know. Believe me, I'm sorry.

I went into my office and dialed my former wife in Long Beach. I had stiffed her on alimony payments for eighteen months. I got a recording that said she was sorry she could not come to the phone but, after all, life was a beach.

Marty came in and dropped the check on my desk.

We're just about even, he said.

VALUED CUSTOMER

My light bill said thank you for your payment, you are a valued customer of Queensboro Lighting. That pleased me. The phone number of my personal representative, William Borden, was on the bill. The bill said I should call him if I had any questions. I called. A woman answered. Mr. Borden was no longer with Queensboro Lighting. Perhaps she could help me? I said that I was a valued customer of Queensboro Lighting and had called to say hello to my representative. She said that was very nice. All their customers were valued, of course, but those who, like myself, realized the importance of paying their bills promptly, were especially valued. Maybe we could meet for lunch, I said. That would be nice, she said but it was against company policy. I understood. She said thank you for calling Queensboro Lighting. Have a nice day.

    A few days later, I got a letter from Queensboro Lighting that thanked me for calling and expressing such warm feelings towards the company and its dedicated employees. The letter said I was an outstanding customer and they looked forward to our continued relationship. It was signed Sheila M. Raynes. I dialed the number on the letter and asked for Sheila M. Raynes. A man said she was in a meeting. Could he help me? I said no, I was replying to a personal letter from Ms. Raynes. He put me on hold and I listened to some nice music. A woman came on. Yes? she said. Is this Sheila M. Raynes? I said. Yes it is, she said. I thanked her for her letter. There was a pause. You wrote, I said, saying that I was an outstanding customer of Queensboro Lighting. Oh, she said, yes. Wouldn't it be nice, I said, if we could meet for lunch and have a chat? She agreed but said the company did not allow such activities during business hours. I said I understood, maybe I should call another time. Sheila M. Raynes lowered her voice. Call after six, she said.

Sheila M. Raynes agreed to have a drink with me. We met in a Japanese restaurant. It was very pleasant with a long wooden bar, subdued lighting and quiet customers. She was small. She had her hair cut short and had wide, engaging blue eyes. She was working towards a degree in communications, she said. She loved her job. She met wonderful people, customers and staff. She wanted to move up and make more money. She wanted to buy a condo and a BMW. I told her about my job in New York Hospital. I was alone, I said. I wasn't ashamed. There was nothing wrong with being alone. It was what I preferred. Yes, that was true, she said, many people live alone and enjoy a full life. It so happened that she was alone just now. She touched my hand. I had an idea. I could cook a little meal. We could get a video. Sheila smiled. We had another drink.

Next morning, I cooked eggs. I poured cognac. I played music while Sheila M Raynes took a shower and walked around my apartment in the nude. I watched her dress. How did she look? she said. She kissed me. I should call. I was her valued lover.

I stopped paying my bills to Queensboro Lighting. I did not call Sheila M. Raynes. I got letters from Queensboro Lighting saying that if there was any problem, I should let them know. I got letters in legal terms, with parts underlined in red, saying that if I did not pay my bill, Queensboro Lighting would find it necessary to terminate my service within ten days. One evening, the phone rang. It was Sheila M. Raynes. She sounded cold, almost angry. I was six months in arrears. Was I experiencing difficulties? Had I lost my job? Was there some problem they could help with? No, I said. The company had been patient and fair, she said. Would I please pay my bill? I said I would if she said she missed me. Please, this is a business matter, she said. These calls were often monitored by supervisors. Say you miss me, I said. She said something in a quavering voice. I can not hear you, I said. Yes, she said, yes, she missed me! Why didn't I call? Why didn't I want to see her? She started crying. Ah, I said and hung up.

That evening, I wrote a check to Queensboro Lighting for the full amount owed. I noted on the bill that once again I looked forward to being their valued customer.

WATER PUMP

I pulled into Ben's garage. There was a low, red car, a Ferrari or a Lotus and a big guy in a peaked cap and plaid jacket. Dan had the hood up.

Shit, the guy was saying. I paint abstractions. You know why? Because I can't draw, that's why!

Ben nodded and gave me a droplight to hold.

The guy looked at me. He had a big jaw. He had small eyes and purple veins in his nose.

Know when I did my best work?

I waited.

When I was sick of it. When I hated it. Hated canvas, hated paint.

Sell any?

He gave me a funny look.

Made a goddamned fortune.

Not bad.

Your ass, not bad! It's all gone too. Every cent. The wife's screaming. The accountant's screaming. Kids starving. House looks like its been bombed.

Ben shut the hood.

Water pump, he said, wiping his hands. He took back the drop light.

The guy ignored him.

You want to know, my wife does a lot of it. Kids too. I come in, mess it up a little, sign it and get it the hell out of my sight.

Give the man a lift? Ben asked. He got in and we drove across the hills, watching the headlights on the road. Christ, he whispered, oh Christ. I dropped him at the Post House. What's that name again? Robbins, he said. Royal Robbins. He slammed the door, turned and stuck his head in the window.

Farm shit before you make art.

When I got home, I went into my son's room, got down one of his art books and looked up the name. He was there all right. His brilliant compositions, the book said, captured the twin currents of atavistic longing and technological abstraction typical of post-modern culture. Hyperkinetic, holistic in its vision, his work re-energized the layered coloring of Gauguin and simultaneously mocked its primitive level of commitment.

I put the book back, poured a drink and went to the window. The street was quiet, the trees dark. Shows what a broken water pump can do to a man.

TRAVELLING THROUGH SPACE

Andrea told me she was pregnant after we made love. I hated to talk after we made love. You don't want it? she said. I said I wanted to become a pilot. You don't want a child? Andrea said. I hated it when she repeated things.

I moved to Tecumseh, New York. Tecumseh used to be called Boxtown. Everyone thought an Indian name would attract tourists. When some Indians started hanging around, everyone wanted Tecumseh to be called Boxtown again.

I worked for the Adventists. The Adventists said the world was going to end in six months. Our job was to keep teenagers away from sex and drugs. It would be easy once they got the news. Every night, I drank, looked for girls. I met Adventists. They were drinking, looking for girls. We had plenty of time, they said, the world wasn't going to end for five or six years.

I drove out to Tecumseh airport. There was a shack with a windsock, a grass runway. A plane was coming in. It was turned to one side. A wing hit the ground. The plane spun around, its propeller kicking up dirt. A smoke ring came out of the engine. I started running. The door of the plane opened and a guy jumped out. He was screaming, his hands covering his face.

Just think, Andrea said, it could have been you. She was going to call her son Thornton. It was an intelligent name, it would make him smarter. Andrea had tried to commit suicide. She slit her wrist and sat in the tub, reading. When nothing happened, she got up and called the police. Maybe we should get married? I said. Oh, thank you, she said.

Andrea worked for a greeting card company. She drew kittens and butterflies all day. At night, she drew genitals on the rejections and left them on the subway. Andrea had no breasts, no hips. Tubular, I said. She liked it that way, she said. One night, her boyfriend rode off on his motorcycle. The next day he was found in a park, sitting on the motorcycle. He was dead.

Our biology teacher at Our Lady of Sorrows High said there was no rational basis for sex. There was no reason why a woman couldn't lay eggs on a rock and a guy come along to fertilize them. That's what fish did. But humans needed to fool around, to pass the time. My uncle Lester was married three times. All he talked about was money.

My buddy Clint had first sex on the subway. This woman grabbed his arm. She was beautiful, an Indian from Columbia. They squeezed against a post. People looked at them from the windows of trains.

The trouble with life, Clint said, was that something better was happening someplace else. Clint was a genius; he was going to be a chemist. One night Clint was in the chemistry lab when it blew up. Everyone said he was making a bomb. The police found him walking along a road, his clothes burned off. When he got out of the hospital, one side of his face was red, like it had been painted.

I had first sex with Melody. She was the batgirl on our baseball team. She had sex with one player a day on a rotating basis. Melody had perfect breasts. My meal ticket, she said, people got famous with less.

In Laramie, I saw a woman sitting on a horse. She looked just like Melody. Hey, Melody, I yelled, rolling down the window, still like ballplayers? The woman smiled. Wheel it home to Queens, Hector, she said.

I went to White Mountain College because I hated schools with names like CUNY or SUNY. Clint said they sounded like sexually transmitted diseases.

Actually there wasn't any white mountain. There weren't any mountains. Far off, you could see some hills. The school was named after this philosopher, Lester White, who died bitter and impoverished. Now all his books are classics.

My roommate was from Tobo, West Virginia. Jared said everyone in Tobo dug coal, everyone was starving and lived in shacks. Every Saturday night, people got drunk and shot one another. Jared's brother got shot in the head. He hears a telephone ringing all the time. Jared had sores on his neck. He was always swigging from a bottle he kept under his pillow. Lots of times, he woke up screaming there was a rat in his bed. One day two guys drove up in a big black car and took Jared away.

Franco Syms, the hockey player, moved in. Everyone called him Baseball because of the stitches on his face. Baseball brought girls home every night. He liked to carry them under his arms, liked to kick open the door wearing a goalie's mask. They undressed, giggling, and then Baseball fell asleep. The girls swore and then got dressed again. That's how I met Jana. She sat on my bed talking in Czech. I sat up, what are you saying? I'm saying, shut up asshole, she said.

Jana had been a speed skater in Czechoslovakia until she got drunk at a Youth Congress and made a speech saying the Czechs were a lost tribe of Eskimos. After that, she lost her skating talent. Jana liked to build igloos, like to pile up furs, drink cognac and make love. She was going to be a veterinarian. She said America was a great country because it snowed all the time.

Jana's father had been killed by a snowplow. He had just come to Tecumseh. He was shoveling snow with Jana when the plow came around the corner and swept him away. The driver was found to be legally insane. People were upset that an insane guy was driving a snowplow. But the autopsy showed that Jana's father had a bad heart. He was going to die soon. Everyone calmed down.

Turner, Jana said, we should marry. She would be a veterinarian, I could be a doctor. We could ski, build igloos, and make love until we were very old. Jana had pills for death. There would be no pain.

I needed time, I needed to think. Sometimes Jana annoyed me. After we had sex, she patted me on the back like I had scored a touchdown. She was always muttering in Czech. What? I'd say. Nothing, she'd say. Then stop it, I'd say.

She'd answer in Czech and we would start again. She liked to eat with her fingers. I hated that. Like a dog, I'd say. What dog? she'd say.

One night, Baseball tried to carry three girls home from a bar, one under each arm and one hanging off his neck. He had ruptured a disk; he was in traction, sandbags against his head.

Around this time, my mother ran away to Florida with Ned Gorman. He was an ex-priest who ran an employment agency called The Second Calling. My father got a cold and six weeks later he was dead. His friend Barney said he died of a broken heart. Barney ran the Trolley Bar. One day he turned on the television in the bar and saw his wife on the *Phil Donahue Show* talking about Women Who Prowl the Malls. He broke the jaw of the first guy who asked for a beer.

Petey talked about collecting stamps. He had been interested in stamps ever since his fifth grade teacher had brought in one from Africa. Mrs Mullins taught the fifth grade for forty years. She had a stroke at her retirement dinner. She was in a home just a few miles from our house. My father talked all the time about going over to see her.

Petey never talked about my mother. Sometimes he did his joke. He'd ask a bus driver, did you call Ernie? He'd meet a homeless guy, shake his hand and say, the midgets have arrived, the socks are in the mail. One Sunday, he stood up in church. The termites are marching, he said. Even the priest laughed. My mother hated his joke, he sounded like a parrot, she said.

My mother always wanted to know what I learned in school. I never told her the good stuff. I liked what Marie Antoinette said. That was cool. I used to wonder what she looked like naked. I used to wonder if they hit on each other in bed the same way we do now. And Dred Scott, I said his name over and over in gym. I asked Ms. Bernard in Readings For Democracy what Dred Scott did after he was freed. That was irrelevant, she said. I told her there was a rock group called Dred Scott. It broke up when the lead guitarist fell down an elevator shaft. Turner, Ms. Bernard said, you're on the cutting edge of stupidity. I liked that. That was my high school quote of all time. And Lee Harvey Oswald, an average guy who made good. Guys with three names always did something important. I used to write Turner Eaton Long and Lee Harvey Oswald over and over. My mother thought I was doing something for English.

My mother went to law school in Florida. That was funny because she had all these freckles. My father said she had so many freckles she was invisible. She wore these big hats like she was riding a buckboard through Kansas. She was always watching courtroom TV, always yelling that the lawyers were morons, she could do better. She wanted to send a rapist to the electric chair because a girl who sat across from her in school had been raped and murdered. The guy who did it got life. Life, my mother yelled, she would have gotten him the chair, thrown the switch. She used to send me postcards with pictures of girls in bikinis. One Christmas, she sent me a picture of herself in a bikini with wreathes over her breasts.

I took my father shopping a week before he died. It was spring. The air was misty. Girls had their coats open. You could hear the crack of baseballs on the high school field. My father stopped to look at a stack of televisions in a store window. They all showed a truck with huge tires climbing over a row of cars. He stood a long time, his hands in his pockets. Turner, he said, what are clowns for?

A guy came into the agency just before we closed. He wore a raincoat, no pants. His legs were purple. He was smiling. He had two teeth. He opened the raincoat and pulled out a gun. Chairs went flying, flesh slapped the floor. There were pops, pink flashes. He shot out the lights. Glass flew like birds. He opened the gun and took bullets out of his pocket. He shot his initials into the walls. Plaster jumped out. Dust floated like fog. He sat down, smiling, the gun on his lap. The cops came. Pardon my bless, he said.

The woman who interviewed me at Summit Tires was pregnant. She kept drinking water, fanning herself with my resume. She asked me what I knew about tires. I liked tires, I said, they smelled good. She took a drink of water. I could see her eye all distended looking at me through the glass. Could I get tires from Akron to Brooklyn? Could I expedite? A guy driving a rig didn't want tractor tires. A guy with four kids in a station wagon didn't want a truck tire. Did I see her point? Was I up to it? It was a challenge, I said but the kind of challenge I liked. She smiled for the first time. A good answer, she said.

I worked with Chet. Chet had been in Nam, had caught shrapnel in his throat. Sometimes he stopped talking. His throat started working. You looked away until it cleared up. When Chet said, but my buddy got killed, he was back in the world.

Chet had a little TV on his desk. It was hard to see what he was looking at. If you tried, he darkened the screen. I expedited tires to Mississippi instead of Brooklyn. Snow tires arrived in Hawaii. Truckers got tractor tires. Tires piled up in places no one knew existed, places like Homespun, Texas. Chet patted my shoulder. I would get the hang of it.

When I told Chet I was quitting, that I was breaking up with Andrea, he said he was sorry. He said we made a good team. He thought we could expedite tires until we retired. We could go bowling, take our kids to picnics, play softball. We could make tapes of all the fun we had. His throat started working. I looked at his little TV. I could see naked girls running around. We shook hands. This fucking world, Chet said, this fucking world.

Andrea called and said she hadn't gotten a check. I said I would turn the matter over to my attorney. She said Thornton was smart. He was going to be a scientist or a doctor. He was going to make a lot of money. Let me know when he discovers the secret of the universe, I said. Fine, she said, but how would you understand it?

No one from White Mountain has ever become famous. A teacher from the Psychology Department had a part in a horror movie. She ran around naked, chased by a garbage compactor which was really the brain of her dead boyfriend. Everyone went to see what she looked like naked. Everyone cheered her breast implants. In her next movie, she was a waitress. She had to look disgusted when this bald guy left her a bad tip. Everyone shouted for her to take her clothes off.

I want to be famous. I don't want to be like Chet, getting hurt in a dumb war, working for thirty years just to get fired. I'd like to travel through space, see what the hell is really going on. Or maybe I could walk around the world and shake hands with everyone. But I think someone has done that. Almost everything has been done. Sometimes I wake up at night thinking about Lee Harvey Oswald. I think, am I going to do something terrible?

ON MARS

It was Wednesday, time to drink. I went to Denny's. A classic. It smelled bad. The blinds were all smashed, hanging crooked in the window. The bartender had a lot of little holes in his cheeks. He had been in the Peruvian army. No one knew what that meant. Any starlets tonight, Pox? I said. You just missed one, Turner, he said. I get home. My wife is leaving me. Lucy left me two, three times a year. I liked it when she left me. I could almost love her. Turner, she said, you're a louse. Dumb. You can't do enough dumb things. That may be, I said, but who's going to clean the house? She slammed the door, sped off in my Honda. I went fishing next morning. Figured it was manly. I went to Mee Lake. Blue sky, blue water, blue hills. God was in his blue period when he got around to the lake. I took out the fishing junk. Stuck the poor bastard of a worm on the hook and tossed him in. Nothing happened. It got boring. Maybe if some fish jumped up and said something in French, it would be better. Maybe if the sky turned green, instead of blue, it would have been better. If the damned birds had said what was on their minds and shut up, it would have been better. I tossed the fishing pole in the lake. Went up to the road. I stuck out my thumb. Why did she always take my Honda? Some girl stopped. Are you nuts? I say. I could be a serial killer. Isn't everyone? she said. Kind of a looker: black hair, blue eyes. But pale skin with little rashes. Her name was Marjorie. Everyone called her Cher. She didn't know why. She was on her way to Syracuse to shoot her mother. Sound funny? Her mother had cancer. Well, in that case, I said. She had a gun. She points to a black bag that says Puma. Years ago, she said, life meant something. People thought they were getting something when they were born. Now, life was no big deal. If all life ended, earth would just be like Mars. She had a point there. We got to my corner. Wow, she says, all her friends live in trailer parks. I invited her in. We could have a drink. She said no thanks but she would definitely look me up on her way back. The house was a mess. The bed was unmade, plates of food lying around. The refrigerator was empty. The tropical fish were eating one another. I called Lucy in Buffalo. She always went to her parents in Buffalo when she left me. Her father answered. He was a cop. He always sounded faggy. I always wondered how he could yell "freeze" and capture a guy sounding like that. Yes, he said, what do you want? Is my wife available or is she in a meeting? I said. Lucy got on the phone. I told her I loved her. Wanted her back. Missed her. She said I was lying. I said we could have fun anyway. She waited for a few seconds and hung up. I was sick of all this shit. I was sick of not having a Honda. I called my buddy Harris. Harris used to steal cars when we were in high school. He was always in counseling. He was always in some juvenile rehab center. His father got an idea. He bought Harris a used car lot. Now Harris was happy. He wore a red plaid shirt every day and talked about camshafts. No one listened. Harris pulled up in his red BMW. I would have a new Honda in no time, he said. He said Lucy always left me when the moon was full. Women were mostly water anyhow. We stopped for a red light by the railroad tracks no one ever saw a train on. Two guys came along. They wore engineer's hats and overalls. One carried a crowbar on his shoulder. The other had a big black wrench in his hand. They came up to the car. The guy with the crowbar pokes out the lights. The wrench guy smashes it down on the hood. It pops up. Paint goes flying. Harris is screaming. He jumps out and the crowbar guy swings. Harris throws out his arm. There's a loud snap. Harris spins against the car, looks up at the sky. The guys walk down the tracks. People come up. A fat guy in a blue shirt hands me a picture of a mountain reflected in a lake. Jesus gave it to him when he was a kid. It brings peace, cures pain. I thank him. He wants a dollar donation. An EMS truck stops. We put Harris in the back. He's blue, sweating. His eyes are bugged. The EMS guy says he is in shock People die from shock. Harris doesn't look like that kind of guy. The EMS guy has had only two hours sleep. Two hours ago he had a burn case. Girl set herself on fire in her parents' backyard. They were getting ready for a barbecue. Now that was funny. Not funny haha but pathologically funny. We get to the hospital. A doctor looks at Harris. He has a complicated fracture. Very serious. He might not regain full mobility of the arm. I see it hanging uselessly by his side. The doctor looks at me. Guys like us think life is television. Well, he's gotta tell us, life is not television. I leave Harris. I take a cab home. The driver is black. I tell him about Harris, about the girl who set herself on fire. It's pathologically funny, I say. The guy stops the car. He turns around. He's a family man, he says. His cab was blessed by the Bishop of Toledo. He doesn't want anyone talking like that in his cab. I tell him I'm just trying to be interesting and informative. There's a car in my driveway. Lucy, I think, but it's not a Honda. It's Cher. She's back from Syracuse. Hey, I say. Yeah, hey, she says. She drove for hours and hours to some place called Poughkeepsie. Some grease jock tells her Syracuse is miles away. Could you believe? She wants to use the facilities, have a drink. It's not like we have to have sex. I make her a martini. We sit around. Cher says she is a sociologist. She's not practicing just now. She does exotic dancing in Centerreach, Long Island. She likes it. She has four, five orgasms a night doing exotic dancing. That's more than a year of regular sex. She's going to write a book about objective eroticism. I say, what's new with your mother? She shrugs. Once you decide not to kill someone you lose interest in them. Yeah, I say. Once I wanted to kill my English teacher. He had this little black moustache that drove me crazy. I bring a knife to school, plan to stick him in the lunchroom. But he has a stroke in the library. When he comes back, I couldn't care less. I even study a little. She looks at me, considering. Had I ever dressed up as a girl? Not to my recollection, I say. She says she's perfectly normal sexually but she needs a trigger. A guy dressed as a girl was a big trigger. I said sometimes I found it hard to start sex because I could imagine it being over. How about taking the gun and getting the punks who hurt my friend? I say. Wow, she says, when she was old and tired, this day would be a big memory. We get in the car and drive into town. We park near the railroad tracks. Cher takes her gun out of the Puma bag. It's small and has a pearl handle. My heart is beating. We wait. We don't see anyone wearing engineer hats and overalls. We drive through town. We pass this guy walking a dog. He's wearing a green beret, has a cigar in his mouth. We laugh. The guy gives us the finger. Cher makes a U at the corner. The guy sees us coming back. He drops the leash and starts running. The dog just stands there. The guy runs into the street. We catch up. Cher sticks the gun out the window. The guy throws out his arms. The cigar falls down the front of his jacket. Bang! we say. Cher drives back to the house. I'm laughing. That was funny, I say. Cher says she never laughs anymore. Everything is funny, so what's the point? We sit in front of the house. Cher says, you going to dress up as a girl or what? She needs to be triggered. Hell, who's going to know? I say. Who's going to care? she says.

THE EASY WAY

Pat retired at fifty-five. He painted the house. He shoveled snow and fixed the roof. In the evening, after dinner, he drank beer and watched television. His son and daughter visited for the holidays. Pat smiled and said little.

His son bought a video camera.

Someday, he said to his wife, he's going to die. I want a memory.

On New Year's Eve, he brought the camera, the lights.

Dad, he said, I'm putting you on tape. Forever. Talk to us.

His father stood up when he saw the lights. He shoved his hands into his back pockets.

Well, listen, he said. I never liked this living. What is it? An urge between the legs? For what? He shrugged. And women. God knows, they talk. They give you the children. They talk. More children. Always children. Food in their mouths, out their bottoms. Sick. Crying. Couldn't wait to get rid of them. You could like them when they leave. Listen now. Take the easy way. Get your job, your television, your beer. You hear? Put your feet up. And ignore them. Ignore the lot of them. It's the easy way.

He waved and sat down.

His son forgot the camera, forgot the lights and stood staring at his father, sitting in brilliant illumination.

SMILING JACK

Jane went to the lady's room when the movie was over. She would only be a minute. I waited in the lobby. People were lining up for the next show. The usher came out of the auditorium carrying a plastic bag full of popcorn cups. He stuffed them into the trashcan, folded his arms and stood looking at the new audience.

We started talking. I told him about a guy I knew in the army. He was a little guy, I said. He wore gold glasses and was always squinting and frowning. He always fainted on road marches, always failed inspection, always pulled KP on weekends. He never talked. The sergeants liked to pick on him. Hey, smiley, hey laughing boy! One called him Smiling Jack. Smiling Jack, why are you always frowning? Why do you always screw up? The name stuck.

We finished basic, I said, and moved to new outfits. Everyone got leave and went home. But Smiling Jack came back to the base in the middle of the night. He broke into the barracks and hanged himself from a rafter over his old cot.

The usher shook his head.

I thought this was going to be a funny story?

I shrugged.

Just a story, I said.

Jane came out of the lady's room. Her eyes were red. She had a tissue in her hand. Theo, she said, I've been thinking. It's over with us. Our relationship is a farce. We're finished. You know it, I know it. I'm in love with Leo. I've called him. He's coming over to pick me up. We're going to his parent's place in New

Hope. This is better, really. It will be friendly. We'll see each other. She kissed me on the cheek. Don't worry, I'll call. She went out the exit door.

Damn, I said.

The usher put his hands to his face.

I can't take this, he said. Tragedy everyday. Sick people, sad people, lonely people. Last week, a guy died in the middle of *Pinocchio*. A young guy.

Listen, he said, putting his hand on my arm. A month ago this friend of mine published a story. He put me in it. All these things were going on, you know, important things. And who am I? He makes me this guy who comes out of a building, lights a cigarette and walks down the street. That's it. That was me, he said. The man in the shadows.

I patted his shoulder. The line of people waiting for the movie had grown. I looked at the crowd and felt afraid.

HOW TO PLAY HARDBALL

The Great Bastard never said good morning. He never said please, never said thanks. The Great Bastard never drank with anyone and never ate with anyone. But everybody said that, deep down, he was Santa Claus. He never showed it.

One day, in the company lunchroom, I overheard two guys plotting to get the Bastard. Nothing new. I called his secretary. When they came back to the office, their desks were gone, Security waiting. I got back to work.

Without warning, his face expressionless, the Great Bastard strode into my office, took a red ball from his pocket and tossed it to me. I jumped up and caught it. We played catch, expanding our distance. We were flawless. We threw harder, faster, grunting with the effort. Neither of us came close to making an error. Then, abruptly, it was over. The Bastard put the ball in his pocket and walked away.

From that day on, he never said good morning. He never said please. And he never said thanks

STOUT ROBERT

I slapped her. I did. I'm sorry.
　　She ran upstairs and I ran after her. Honey. Dee, that was her nickname. She went into the bedroom and locked the door. She was crying and it made me feel bad. Eight years married and we hardly ever had a quarrel.
　　In fifteen minutes, I hear a car. The doorbell. It's her dad. His gray hair is standing up. His eyes red and watery, as usual. If only I had my strength, he says, waving his fist. I'm thinking, he's going to have a stroke and then what. I apologize. I tell him it never happened before. I tell him how much I love his daughter. His mouth moves. He's searching for words. Trying to express the inexpressible. You're a shipwreck, he's says. I told her not to get on. You're a hooligan. I can't help it, I laugh. He spits on my shoes.
　　The door of the bedroom opens. She comes out. My darling, my beanpole. Too tall, too thin, her blond head shaved. Those green eyes, famous lips. I run to her and start apologizing. She lifts her chin, her eyes blinking real fast. You hit me, you skunk, she says. I stand back. It was her telling me I smelled which started the whole thing and which for one instant, one tiny instant, caused me to forget how much I loved her. Forget love, I said, I adore you. She considered, her hand moving to her cheek where, I regret to say, there is a mark like the imprint of a glove. You're a smelly skunk, she said, spitting the words at me.
　　What I did was, as soon as she left, I got into my car and drove into town for a drink. While I could by no means be considered an alcoholic—I held down a job, never had blackouts and got silly, never belligerent—I was a member of that fraternal group. Funny, Dee never complained about that. Besides, I thought that

everyone liked stories of a wife leaving a husband and I looked forward to telling it because while I was a good guy and one of the boys, I wasn't one of the more popular boys for reasons that remain obscure.

I'm driving along, trying to fix the radio to a new age station because that is the kind of music Dee likes, when I see this dog. It is red and running along the shoulder of the road, its mouth lolling, looking like a wolf or a coyote. The next thing I know, its tail goes between its legs and it darts under my car. Oh God, I cry! I wait to hear the horrible howling, the crunch of bones. My heart is breaking.

I get out. I don't see any dog and I think, thank you God. But, then I see it, in the grass by the side of road. I run up to it. Please be dead. Don't look up to me with your pleading eyes. There is no blood but its bushy tail is black. Its hindquarters look hard and stuck together. It's panting and when I come close, it lifts its head. His eyes are tender and sad. My throat hurts. I have little to do with animals. But I like them. They have a tougher time than we do. I believe that. But I don't deserve this. Cars are speeding by. The dog's fur stands up every time like it's a pleasant breeze. A pickup stops. A guy looks out the window. He's wearing a hat like a cop or a guard. He's got a straw in his mouth. I start to explain and he says, pick him up. I can't, I say. You can, he says, pick him up. I say, what if I hurt it? What if it bites me? The guy shakes his head and drives off. I approach the dog. It tries to lift its head but it can't. Ah, Christ, I say, I'm sorry. I put my hands under him gently and the dog growls. Oh, shit. Cars are whizzing by. Tractor-trailers going like comets. If I don't do something someone is going to kill me. I'm thirty-seven years old and have great expectations of my life.

Well, I get it done. Get him in the back seat, frankly expecting to get blood and entrails and shit all over me. But the poor creature is going into shock. I learned that when my father died, sitting in his armchair looking at television and all the time he's in shock. I put him down on the seat and no sooner get behind the wheel then he lets out a howl that made my hair stand on end. God, I shout! Oh, God! Why does this have to be? And why aren't we trained for emergencies? Suppose it was Dee? My little Irish mother who wouldn't hurt a fly? I look back at the dog. His eyes are staring and very white.

I drive into town. Don't die, I say over and over. Please don't die. I get over to Doc Estes' office. Doc is a good guy. A Marine captain, played football at Colgate. He has a problem much worse than mine in that he will walk out of his office to get a pack of cigarettes and turn up a week later in Cooperstown or Delhi not remembering a thing and certain that he has ruined his life. Once, he actually married some teenager. His wife's family had to pay a lot of money to put it to rest. Minny is his wife, his nurse and receptionist. A small woman with ample breasts and hips who was beautiful once and actually danced at Radio City Music Hall and for six months had been the girlfriend of a real estate magnate who woke up one morning and threw her out. Esty said she was amazing. Always cheerful and smiling, no matter what the circumstances, except for what Esty called her times when she would stop talking almost in mid-sentence. That went on for a day or two, once for a whole week, before she would start talking again. Exactly where she left off, Esty swore.

I run into the office which has a Chinese restaurant on one side, a dry cleaner on the other. There are a few people I pay no attention to, the types who look like their animals. I run up to the desk. Minny doesn't understand and looks shocked. She thinks I ran over a person. I explain again. Where's the dog? she says finally. Outside in the car, I tell her. You picked her up? I know immediately I did something wrong, yet before I have time to worry, she picks up the phone. Esty, she says, send Solly out here. In a nano second, this kid comes busting out of the back where the examining rooms are. His hair is forest black, like Esty's. He has a beard the color of night and is wearing suspenders, like Esty. The strange thought arrives in my mind that he is Esty's son but I never knew he had a son. It shows you how much you know about people. Minny explains that he needs something. It has a technical name. The kid runs back in the direction he came from and comes back so fast I wonder if he had left in the first place. He's holding something that looks like a sling for a broken arm. Where's the patient? he says, just like Esty would.

It's not like I run over a dog every day, I say, running out to the car with him. It's not like there's time to practice. But Solly ignores me. He's on a mission. He opens the door and gets the dog into the sling in no time, hardly looking at him or saying a word. The dog doesn't resist, his head lolling, his eyes white. I can't stand the idea of his dying.

When we come back into the office, the people look at me like I'm a serial killer doing his perp walk. I don't care what it costs, I tell Minny, I want the dog fixed. Somehow it comes out that I just had a big fight with Dee and she left me. Minny smiles. Deirdre is such a lovely girl, she says. She's too good for you, Gregory. I sit down. I think, maybe I should leave this stupid town and start a new life. The woman next to me who is wearing overalls like she had just dug up the cabbage patch, turns conspicuously in the other direction. I get up. I think I will go and have a drink to help me calm down, I say. Minny hates that because of Esty and his well-known problems. Everybody glares.

I walk to the Home Inn. Everyone calls it the Home Run. No one knows how that started. The name was meant to suggest a cozy and congenial place. It's filled with characters, best left to the imagination. The current bartender is Homer. You can imagine the confusion that causes. He's a big guy, wide shoulders, lantern jaw, always sunburned because he's always out fishing or hunting. Two years ago, he had a famous encounter with a black bear he stared down with a wooden leg he found hanging on a tree. I had my Scotch and told Homer my story. He shook his head. Big mistake, Gregg. You should have left him, he says. You see, the brain secretes this chemical. It's a natural tranquilizer. They die a peaceful death. Wouldn't feel a thing. Dolly Pickens was listening. She liked to sit, smiling into her Manhattan, eavesdropping on everyone's conversations. She wore a regular flowered dress with a flower in her hair like a femme fatale in an old movie. Homer, she said, he'll need a tranquilizer when he gets the bill from Doc Esty. She laughed. She had a real sour laugh. For some reason, she didn't like me. She never looked at me when she spoke to me. She looked at someone else as though I was in quarantine. You know the trouble with you, Gregory? she said, staring into her Manhattan like there was a microphone in it. I could see she had something in mind. A big put down. The trouble with you is you spent seven years in a monastery. Three, I said. And it wasn't a monastery, I scoffed. I was studying to be a priest. She laughed. He doesn't get the point, she said to Homer. He doesn't know enough about women, that's the problem with him. Homer said nothing. He turned on the hockey game and we all shut up.

I finished my drink. Homer reached for the Scotch bottle. I put my hand over my glass. I have to go, I said. You ever have a tumor? Homer said. Jesus, no, I said. Why? Homer was worried. His wife had a tumor. He hesitated. He was looking at me but I could tell he was talking to Dolly. What am I, a two-way radio? His wife has a tumor on her pelvis. Was that bad did I know? I didn't so I left him to trash it out with Dolly.

Minny had gone home. Esty was waiting, sitting in her chair, his glasses up on his head, wearing his white coat which had a lot of stains on it the origin of which I didn't want to think about. He looked glum, the way he usually did after a day of telling little kids the bird they found in the backyard had gone to heaven. I guess I knew. The dog died, I suppose? I said. Esty nodded. He said everything that could have been broken was. Everything that could have been crushed was. You did a good job, Gregg my boy. I didn't take it personally. I knew the way he was. It wasn't my fault, you know, I said. Esty nodded, closing his eyes so long I thought he wasn't going to open them again. You want to have a drink? he said. I looked at my watch. I can't, I said, I have a problem with Dee. Yeah, he said, Minny told me. What the hell do you see in that woman?

I get home. I'm not stupid. I see my chance and I get on the phone with Dee. Dee was a very softhearted person. That was one of the things I liked about her. I tell her the whole story. Pretty soon, she's crying. You did everything you could? she said. I did, I said. And it didn't suffer, did it Gregg? Not a bit, I said, telling her how a chemical kicks in and takes away any pain. Baby, I say, making my voice as soft as possible, reminding myself of the confessional. Come home. I'm not a brute. You know that. I'm sorry for everything. I'm sorry, sorry, sorry. You don't mean that, she said. You love to hear yourself talk, Gregg. You think you have the gift of gab. I told her I would never, ever raise a hand to her again. May God burn my soul, I said. I was thinking. Thinking real fast. Dee, I say. We could start a new life. Get out of New York. We could move to California. I could go back to college. Finish my degree. I could become a teacher like I always wanted to. You could get a better job. Oh, Dee. Just think. A little house by the beach. Maybe Venice? California? Dee said. Why not? I said. Darling, I love you. We could be happy again. I know we could. You don't mean it, Dee said.

I danced around with happiness. That was her way of giving in. The best thing would be to clean up. Shower and shave, whatever. The washing. That's what started us going in the first place. Wine when she came home, nice romantic music on. Make love, slow and careful. I think in the shower, maybe it was meant to be, maybe there was some plan. When I'm finished getting cleaned up, I stand in front of the mirror. Shaved, with my hair combed, my mustache trimmed, I'm a good-looking guy. Sometimes I wonder why I don't turn the girls' heads more. I put on one of the expensive shirts Dee got me when it looked like I was going to get promoted at work, my best pair of chinos and loafers which needed polishing but I figured we weren't going to spend a lot of time examining my shoes. Lots of cologne which Dee loved. I was scrubbing my teeth when the bell rings. Perfect, I think, running downstairs and throwing open the door. But it's not Dee. It's some guy. A weird looking guy, skinny, wire glasses twisted all over his face. He's scratching at his face, dancing around. You son of a bitch! he screams. You killed Stout Robert! Stout Robert! My dog, my friend! We went everywhere together! We did everything together! You took him away from me! And, you know what? I'm going to kill you! Whoa, I say. Whoa, you got this wrong. This is for Stout Robert, he shouts and comes this roundhouse punch. I saw it sure, but it is one thing to see it, another to get out of the way. The punch caught me square on the cheekbone. I saw this flash, this yellow star they draw in comic books and suddenly I'm sitting down. And the guy is dancing on the lawn, looking back at me, laughing.

As if that wasn't bad enough, Deirdre took my advice. She went to California. She went back to school and got a house in Venice. Only she did it without me, of course. But you know what? Ever since that day, when I see a dog, any dog, my heart goes out to him.

LITTLE DARLINGS

The fish was dead, upside down in the plants it had taken her months to grow. Alice lifted him out with a net. His eyes were open. She felt a pang. What had she done?

She sat on the train, the newspaper in her lap. He was a beautiful fish, silvery, black eyed, trailing long fins. She had bought him two years ago. He was as big as her fingernail. They can live a long time, Tom in Marine World had said, but it's hard. You have to be careful.

She told Irene. They had tea and scones every morning before work. Irene had a dog, Finn. She kept a picture of him on her desk. A huge thing with a dark face, a wet, loose mouth. Her daughter made films somewhere and lived with a succession of men who drank and sent her home crying. He was beautiful, Alice said, I killed him. Irene shrugged. It's just a fish. You were upset when Finn was sick, Alice said. Irene rolled her eyes. Dogs have feelings. You can't compare a dog to a fish. You should have children, a nice dog, like everyone else. Irene shivered. Fish are creepy. Alice sipped her tea, observing her friend with her large, cool eyes.

Alice went to Marine World after work. She liked the creaking of the wood floors, the brilliant tanks, the dense animal smell mixed with disinfectant. Tom wore his leather cap, a black t-shirt with the sleeves ripped away at the shoulders. He had been a road manager for a rock group. His mustache was turning gray. A man with tattoos on his arms was buying a parrot which barked in protest. Alice went straight to the Cichlid tank. She watched them swim by, their black eyes moving slightly. Two young ones hid in the grass. So, Tom said, walking up behind her, you want a fish? With customers like you, I can retire. Alice smiled her thin smile, one hand holding her coat closed. My Cichlid died, she said. Tom smoothed his mustache. How long you have him? Two years. Good. That's good for a Cichlid. She tried to explain. I didn't know, she said, her eyes drifting to the tank. I'm so sad. He put his hand on her shoulder. I understand. She could smell his after-shave, like disinfectant, she thought. You know, a fish is no substitute, you know what I mean? Alice moved so that his hand fell away. She put her finger on the glass. That one, she said. I like his eyes. You like his eyes, Tom mimicked, picking up his net. Which one? She pointed again. You said the other one. You can't make up your mind?

She carried the fish home in a plastic bag filled with water. Raymond was tending the door. He lived in the basement, in a steaming room next the boiler with a broken couch, a discarded bed, pictures of naked women on the walls. He was bald, his face splotched with broken veins. He had cages of birds, a hamster, three dachshunds. He looked at the fish and smiled. Alice told him what had happened. A death in the family, let me tell you. My bird die, he threw up his hands, I can't think about it. Can't sleep, it makes me so sad. Little darlings, that's what they are. Alice touched his arm.

She unlocked her apartment and, without taking off her coat, set the plastic bag in the water. The fish grew excited, butting his head against the invisible wall. Alice smiled. Soon, my dear. She put her coat in the closet and, rubbing her hands, stood in front of the answering machine. There were no messages. The doorbell rang. She looked carefully through the peephole at Raymond. He was smiling, holding something above her line of vision. She opened the door and he thrust a cage at her in which two finches sat fluttering. These sweets, they'll cheer you up, he said. Alice stepped back, folding her arms across her chest. Six days old. Cost a fortune in the store. Oh, they're lovely, Raymond but I can't. I have fish. His eyes moved nervously. Fish and birds, they don't get along. I never hear that, he said softly. Alice shook her head. They just don't. He looked at his finches. You saying you don't want them? I can't, Raymond. He nodded and walked away.

Alice shut the door and locked it. She went to the tank and released the fish. She leaned close to the glass, her eyes large and shimmering, watching him dart back and forth. In time, he swam calmly, aware of her presence.

HERE'S LOOKING AT YOU

I'm on the train heading to work. Guy beside me wants to talk. How can you let this happen? he says. Killing dolphins just to catch tuna. Killing elephants just to get tusks. Burning down the rain forests just to get timber. The world is being polluted. The ozone layer is dispersing. Everyone will get skin cancer. AIDS is a plague. Drugs are destroying children. Every two minutes, some guy kills his wife. Tell me, how can you let this happen? I'm glad when the train gets in. I'm glad to hurry off to work. Don't want to think about these things.

Next morning, guy is back on the train. Got some woman buttonholed. I see his mouth going, can read his lips. He's up to ozone layer when the woman gets up. Walks back and sits down next to me. I look at her. She smiles. Yeah, I say, sat next to him yesterday. Ah, she says. Well, you know, he's right. Yes, he's right, I say. She takes out her *Wall Street Journal*. Turns to an article about car sales. I open up *The Times*. Turn to the sport pages. She looks at me. She smiles. Well, she says, here's looking at you.

IN DORIAN'S OFFICE

— He spent a fortune trying to remove every blemish from her ass.

— Just before orgasm, her face became grave.

— Try to think of existence as another form of television.

— When I'm alone with the cat, the two of us sit looking at the door.

— For him, life was a slow leak in the engine room.

— He always waited for her breasts to touch the eggs.

— When she died, a portion of North America grew quieter.

— Sundays at home put an end to his greatness.

— She always limped after they had quarreled.

— She loved the nights he turned criminal.

— She said, soon, if you don't mind, I will take a bite of you.

— His talk of greatness made me think of peas falling into a pot.

— A fly must feel that he is constantly doing something wrong.

— I've always wanted to organize the crumbs.

— He made love as though poring over a map.

—In Cincinnati, she reasoned, the men were broken hearted.

MOTION PICTURE

After ten years, she said, throw it out. It was a picture of a seagull on a pier they had bought from a student in Zurich.

He put it in the incinerator room. A few minutes later, there was a knock on the door. It was a tall man with a graying beard.

I sold this picture to you in Zurich, ten years ago, he said. My wife died a few weeks later. Grief stricken, I got into a fight in a bar and was badly knifed. I went to live in Germany and worked in an auto parts plant. That was not for me, so I married a barmaid and stayed home. She bore me blond twins, a boy and a girl. I loved them more than life. I searched for the woman's savings, stole them and took the children to America. Since that time, I have been working as a waiter and going to school to study photography, after all. Tonight I was visiting a woman who had been kind to me in Dresden. She is very ill. I took her bandages, her medicine to the incinerator. I found the picture and visited two of your neighbors before finding you. He smiled, presented the picture and walked away.

What was that his wife asked?

He told her the story. She returned the picture to its place on the wall and they never mentioned it again.

CONEY ISLAND SHOOT

I sit near Kimberly. She's perfect, tall, blond, pretty. She's going to be a doctor. She talks about the ozone, the economy. No one listens.

Russia swims all day, jetty to jetty. She puts cream on her body, eats yogurt. She came to America. She worked, went home. People asked, what did you do? What do you mean do? No one liked her. She decided America is the land of do. She swims all summer, skis all winter. Now she has enough do. Everyone likes her.

Ron works a fishing boat out of Sheepshead Bay. He puts worms on hooks, pulls in parts of bodies wrapped in plastic. He hits on the single girls. Might I join you? He has standards. Dress clean. Don't talk sex. Don't stare. She says walk, smile. Say, have a nice life.

Edson humps beer, the pretzels. He won't go in the water. It's full of sharks. He's sold drugs. He's gotten stabbed, been in the slammer. This is the toughest. The worst. He's in love with Kimberly. Gives her a pretzel every day. See any sharks?

Doc's the lieutenant. He teaches in Aviation High. Sometimes he can hear the cries of people who have drowned. His wife is a doctor. She had a breakdown.

Worked too hard, worried too much. She sits on the boardwalk, holding a black umbrella, waving.

The wetheads come to the beach when it rains. When there's thunder over Sandy Hook. Blowfish, Kimberly says. Edson sits under her chair singing Frank Sinatra songs. I see three movies. Doc only reads when it rains. He started *Bonfire of the Vanities* last summer. He's half way through. Russia calls Russia. Ron looks in museums for the girls who didn't come to the beach. The guards scare him, the paintings scare him. My wife is on the answering machine. She's leaving me. Go to Toxic Beach and rot.

It's cold. White caps out to the horizon. Kimberly is wrapped in a blanket watching Russia do her laps. She jumps up, blows her whistle. An old lady is waving near the jetty. Kimberly hits the sand. She drags the woman out by her arms. She was looking for crabs. She's hungry. She's drunk.

Chan's is under the elevated subway. Everyone in Chan's is a crook. Everyone in Chan's has been in jail. You order it, they steal it. You pay what they say. Chan did ten for armored car robbery. Greatest day of his life. He killed a guy in Oswego. The guy jumped him out of an alley, broad daylight. Chan threw a headlock on him. Something snapped. The guy went limp. Chan dumped him and ran. He thinks about it sometimes.

Sweet and Ho work the garbage truck. Sweet goes to Pratt. He's building a giant mouth. What America is all about. It's going to make him famous. He never eats, never sleeps. He's in the Zone. Things are in slow motion, birds hang in the sky, voices come down a tube from the sun. A day in the Zone is a year of regular life. Ho laughs, drinks beer. He has no ambition. He wants to be a Ranger. Wants to drive the green jeep up and down the beach throwing up waves of sand.

Thelma was hit by a bike. Knocked her down the stairs into the sand. Everyone ran. Doc picked up her shoe. My bird, my little bird. She looked dead.

Fourth of July, sand like the Sahara. Edson runs out of beer. People sit blanket to blanket. Blaster wars, drinking. Doc stands by the jetty. He can tell people who want to drown by the way they walk to the water. A girl puts down a chair.

She looks fourteen. She smiles, peels off her clothes. I'm excited. Her father arrives, glares. I say, Senor, I'm waiting for my gay friend, Ron.

The fish are dead, the plants black. Bags of garbage fill the kitchen, the foyer. I call Kelly. She flies a Piper tow plane out of Redbank. She wanted to be a lawyer. Before that, a poet. Before that, a veterinarian. She read a book about Amelia Earhart. She dreamed about her every second night. She became a pilot. She wears a leather jacket, a scarf. She dips her wings when she flies over Coney. There's nothing at Coney Island, I say. No book, no movie. It's a failure. Everything fails, Kelly says. Rome failed, Communism failed. Ernest Hemingway killed himself. Mars dried up. New York is dying. The United States is dying. She's going to crash. I'm going to be a drunk.

Ron shows up on Saturday. He's in a family colony. Rows of blankets, umbrellas, kids dumped like buddas. The husbands pop cans of beer, the wives open baskets of food. Ron's wife is screaming, the kid is screaming. Sweet and Ho stop the truck. The single girls sit up. Ron blushes.

Ho couldn't sleep. He drove to Brighton. Sat on the beach, listening to the water slap the jetties, seeing big stars. Something flew over the water. It didn't make a sound. It had a row of lights. Ho figured it was a space ship. The guy driving it couldn't sleep. Just wanted to see the beach.

Mindy M and Mindy D live in a condo on Ocean Parkway. D is a college professor. She wears dainty glasses, reads books all day. M brings little sandwiches, Perrier water. She takes D's hand, leads her to the water. D splashes her arms, her face. M dries her with a little towel. Ron hit on D when M was sleeping. Go away, M said, or I'll break your spine.

Lizard Man is skinny. He wears a jock-strap suit. He squats on his blanket. He lifts an arm, a leg. He throws his head back. He gets up, stands on one leg, arms extended. A lizard, Doc says, he should stick his tongue out. His eyes follow all the women, Kimberly says.

Goines shows up. He was in the papers. He tried to kill his wife. Only she had to die happy. After they made love. After a party. After a big surprise. Only Goines and his wife never made love. They never went to parties. The only surprise she had was when her mother dropped dead and fell through the Christmas tree. Someone told the police. They put Goines on trial. The jury acquitted him. No one could be that nice. Some muscle guy covered with oil walks over to Goines. We don't want murderers on our beach. Goines shrugged, picked up his stuff.

Thelma's back on the boardwalk. She's got a nurse, a wheelchair, a red umbrella. She waves, we all jump up and wave like crazy.

We're drinking beer, tossing the cans in the air. Fog sits off shore. The water is flat and gray. Kimberly talks Edson into a swim. He's shaking. He holds her hand. They go straight out. Edson starts screaming. Something touched him! He throws up his arms, slips away from Kimberly. Doc dives in. Guards push off the catamaran. They tow Edson in, lie him on the sand. He's convulsed, vomiting foam. Kimberly is crying. No one looks at her.

Sweet and Ho walk up to Lizard Man. You look weird man. My wife, Lizard says. Every inch has got to be tan, like mahogany. All summer he drowns in love. Winter is bad. She calls him a mushroom. Won't look at him. Gotta get it when you can.

Kelly takes off, gets her nose up. She stalls, flips over, hits a tree. Her banner falls across a house. The wings give way. She falls to the street. A guy in the house opens a window and starts screaming. Cars drive on the sidewalk to get around her. Kelly starts kicking out the windshield. A guy on a bicycle stops. You better have insurance, he says.

Labor Day, we go to Chan's. We exchange phone numbers, promise to get together. Doc makes a toast. Walt Whitman said there never can be more life than there is in the present. You understand that, you understand the beach. Whitman was in the Zone, Sweet says. Kimberly has decided to become an actress. The criminals start hitting on her. Edson shows up. He's going back to school, going to become a doctor. Chan says we're a bunch of suckers. The last boy scouts. Kelly comes in dressed like Amelia. She looks cute with her blond bangs and green eyes. She's going to marry me, she says. She has a thing about failure. The book, they yell, where's the book? Another summer, I say, another summer.

THE LAST MAN

It was my thing. I got up at the last minute, got the last train. I bought the last newspaper. I rode in the last car and was usually the last off. Who cared? I was the last person anyone would notice, would confide in, would suspect, blame or get interested in. My parents used to say I was the last guy they would worry about. I was the last guy women flirted with, the last guy men admired. I finished last in my graduation class.

So, one day I was surprised when two guys stopped me and handed me a sign. It was wood, shaped like a crucifix and said THE LAST MAN in red letters. I liked that. I took it to work and put it next to my desk. No one paid attention. I was the last person to have a sense of humor or do anything bizarre. I had a regular day. Nothing special happened. You know why. But when I started for home, people were lined up in the streets. The line stretched for blocks. No one knew where it started, where it was going. I got on the line with my sign. A cop saw me and stuck out his hand. That's it, he said, he's last.

We crossed midtown. We walked to the George Washington Bridge. It took hours. I looked back. The city was dark. No lights, no cars, no airplanes, no sound. Something was wrong. The world's busiest city, shut like a movie house. Whatever had happened, I would be the last to know.

978-0-595-35806-9
0-595-35806-3

Printed in the United States
32741LVS00008B/556-564